the composition

Text copyright © 1998 by Antonio Skármeta
Illustrations copyright © 2000 by Alfonso Ruano
English translation copyright © 2000 by Elisa Amado
Originally published in Spanish as *La composición* by Ediciones Ekaré, Caracas, Venezuela in 2000.
First English-language edition 2000

Groundwood Books / Douglas & McIntyre
720 Bathurst Street, Suite 500, Toronto, Ontario M5S 2R4

Distributed in the USA by Publishers Group West
1700 Fourth Street, Berkeley, CA 94710

We acknowledge the support of the Canada Council for the Arts, the Ontario Arts Council and the Government of Canada through the Book Publishing Industry Development Program for our publishing activities.

Canadian Cataloguing in Publication Data
Skármeta, Antonio
The composition
Translation of: La composición.
A Groundwood book.
ISBN 0-88899-390-0
1. Dictatorship — Juvenile fiction. I. Ruano, Alfonso. II. Title.
PQ8098.29.K3C613 2000   j863   C99-932781-X
PZ7.S626C9 2000

Printed and bound in China by Everbest Printing Co. Ltd.

the composition

Antonio Skármeta
pictures by Alfonso Ruano

Groundwood Books   Toronto   Vancouver   Buffalo

PEDRO was disappointed. His parents had given him a soccer ball for his birthday, but he had wanted a white leather ball with black patches, like the ones real soccer players used, not this plastic thing with blue spots.

"When I want to make a header, this ball just floats away. It feels like a bird, it's so light!" he protested.

"So much the better," answered his father. "This way you can't hurt your head and get dizzy."

He gestured to Pedro to be quiet because he wanted to hear the radio. For the past month, the streets had been filled with soldiers. Now Pedro noticed that every night his father would settle into his favorite spot on the sofa. Then he and Pedro's mother would adjust the antenna on the radio and listen carefully. Sometimes friends joined them. They sat on the floor, smoking like chimneys, with their heads pressed to the green box.

"Why are you always listening to that noisy radio?" Pedro asked his mother.

"Because it's interesting," she answered.

"What does it say?"

"Things about us, about our country."

"What things?" Pedro asked again.

"Things that are happening."

"How come it's so hard to hear?" he demanded.

"The voices are a long way away," his mother answered.

Pedro looked sleepily out the window, trying to guess from which of the faraway hills the voices could be coming.

In October Pedro became the star of the neighborhood soccer games. Sometimes he played with his friends along a deliciously shaded street. It was as cool as swimming in a river in summer. Pedro felt as though he were in a stadium roofed with murmuring leaves that applauded as he took a pass from his friend Daniel, whose father, Don Daniel, owned the local grocery store. Like the great star Pele, Pedro snuck through the giant defencemen and shot straight through the posts for a goal.

"I scored," yelled Pedro, and he ran to hug his teammates. They lifted him onto their shoulders, because even though he had just turned nine, he was small and light.

"Why are you so little?" they teased him.

"Because my father is small and my mother is small," Pedro said.

"Probably your grandfather and grandmother are, too, because you are so, so tiny."

"I'm little, but I'm smart and fast. The only thing that's fast about you guys is your mouth," Pedro retorted.

One day, when the boys were playing on the street, Pedro rushed on goal. He ran up to Daniel, who was the goaltender. Pedro faked a shot, and when Daniel leaped forward to intercept the ball, Pedro gently kicked it over him through the two pebbles that served as goalposts.

"Goal!" screamed Pedro. He waited for his friends' applause. But no one was paying any attention. Everyone was staring at Don Daniel's grocery store.

Up and down the street, windows were opening. People were craning around the corner to see. Some doors slammed shut. Then Pedro saw what everyone else was looking at. Daniel's father was being dragged down the street by two men. A group of soldiers were pointing machine guns at him. When Daniel tried to approach his father, a soldier pushed him back.

"Calm down," said the soldier.

Don Daniel looked at his son. "Take care of the store for me," he said.

As the soldiers pushed him toward a jeep, Don Daniel tried to put his hand in his pocket. Immediately a soldier raised his machine gun.

"Careful!" he shouted.

"I want to give my son the keys to the store," Don Daniel said.

A soldier grabbed his arm. "I'll do it," he barked.

The soldier felt Don Daniel's pockets. When he heard a jingle, he pulled out the keys and threw them. Daniel caught them. The jeep pulled away, and the mothers who had been standing in their doorways ran out, grabbed their children by their collars and pushed them into their houses.

Pedro stood by Daniel in the swirling dust that the jeep had stirred up as it drove off.

"Why did they take him?" Pedro asked.

Daniel pushed his hands into his pockets and squeezed the keys.

"My father is against the dictatorship," he said.

Pedro had heard these words before on the radio at night. But he didn't really understand them.

"What does that mean?" he asked.

Daniel looked at the empty street and whispered, "They want the country to be free. For the army not to be the government."

"They arrest people for that?" asked Pedro.

"I think so," answered Daniel.

"What are you going to do?" asked Pedro.

"I don't know," said Daniel.

A neighbor came up and ran his hand through Daniel's hair. "I'll help you close up," he said.

Pedro walked off dribbling his ball. Since there was no one around to play with, he ran across the street to wait for the bus that would bring his father home from work.

When his father arrived, Pedro hugged him. His father leaned down and gave him a kiss.

"Isn't your mother back yet?" he asked.

"No," answered Pedro.

"Did you play much?"

"A little," said Pedro.

His father held Pedro's head tight against his chest.

"Soldiers came and took Daniel's father away," said Pedro.

"I know," said his father.

"How do you know?" asked Pedro.

"They called me on the phone and told me."

"Daniel owns the store now," said Pedro. "Maybe he'll give me some candy."

"I don't think so," said his father.

"They took Don Daniel away in a jeep just like the ones in the movies," said Pedro.

His father didn't say anything. He breathed deeply and looked sadly down the street. Even though it was still light, the only people out were men coming slowly home from work.

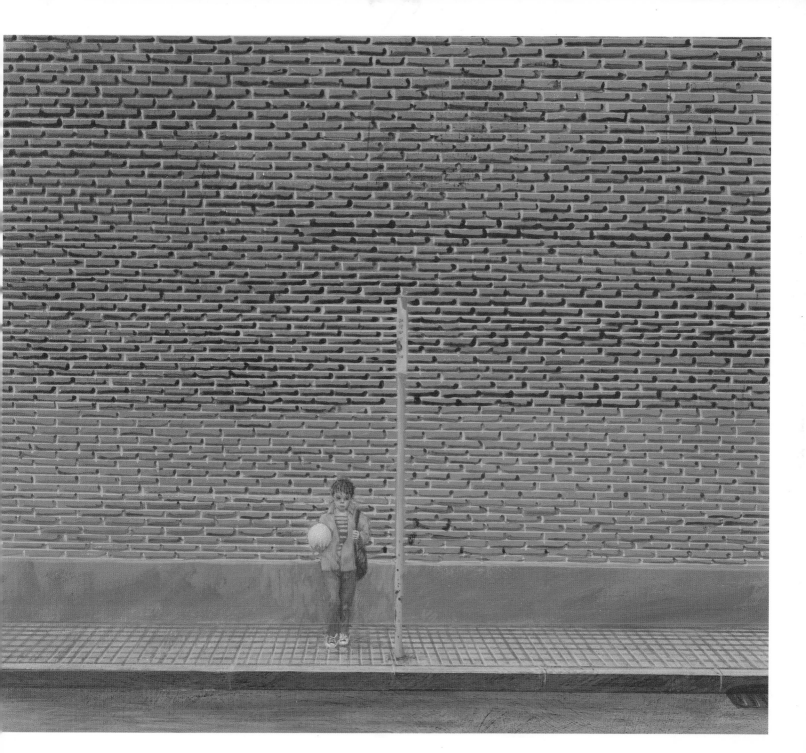

"Do you think it will be on TV?" asked Pedro.

"What?" asked his father.

"Don Daniel."

"No."

That night Pedro sat down to eat with his mother and father. Even though no one told him to be quiet, Pedro didn't say a word. His parents ate without speaking, either.

Suddenly, his mother started to cry silently.

"Why is my mother crying?" asked Pedro.

His father looked first at Pedro and then at Pedro's mother, but he said nothing.

"I'm not crying," his mother said.

"Did someone do something to you?" asked Pedro.

"No," she answered.

They finished their supper in silence and Pedro went to put on his pajamas. When he came back to the living room, he saw that his parents were hugging each other on the sofa. Their heads were bent close to the radio, which was making strange sounds. It was hard to hear what they were because the volume was turned down very low.

"Father, are you against the dictatorship?" Pedro asked quickly.

His father looked at his son, then at his wife, and then they both looked at Pedro. His father slowly nodded.

"Will they take you to jail, too?" Pedro asked.

"No," said his father.

"How do you know?" said Pedro.

"Because you bring me luck," smiled his father.

Pedro leaned against the door frame, pleased that he wasn't being sent off to bed as usual. He paid attention to the radio, trying to understand it. When the radio said, "the military dictatorship," Pedro felt as if all the pieces that had been floating around loose in his head were coming together like a jigsaw puzzle.

"Father," he said, "am I against the dictatorship?"

His father looked at Pedro's mother as though the answer to the question might be written in her eyes. His mother scratched her cheek with a funny look and said, "I can't say."

"Why not?" asked Pedro.

"Children aren't against anything," she said. "Children are just children. They have to go to school, study hard, play and be good to their parents."

Usually when Pedro heard long sentences like this he stayed quiet. But this time, with his eyes still firmly fixed on the radio, he said, "Okay, but if Daniel's father is in jail, Daniel won't be able to go to school."

"Go to bed, son," said his father.

The next day, Pedro ate two pieces of toast with jam, washed his face and ran to school as fast as he could so he wouldn't be late. On the way, he saw a blue kite caught in a tree, but no matter how high he jumped, he couldn't reach it.

The bell was still ringing when the teacher walked into the classroom. She was walking stiffly. A man wearing a military uniform strode beside her. He had a medal pinned to his chest, a gray mustache and dark glasses, darker than the dirt on Pedro's knee after a soccer game.

"Stand up very straight, children," the teacher said.

The children stood up. The soldier smiled under his toothbrush-shaped mustache and his dark glasses.

"Good morning, my young friends," he said. "I am Captain Romo and I'm here on behalf of the government, that is to say, General Perdomo, to invite the children in this school to write a composition. The child who writes the very best one will receive a gold medal and a sash in the colors of the flag from General Perdomo's very own hand. The winner will also carry the flag in the Patriot's Week parade."

Captain Romo put his hands behind his back, gave a little jump and straightened his neck, lifting his chin a little. "Attention! Sit down!"

The children obeyed.

"All right," said the captain. "Take out your notebooks. Notebooks at the ready? Take out your pencils. Pencils at the ready? Write! Title of the composition? What my family does at night. Understand? That is to say, what you and your parents do from the moment you get home from school and work. Which friends come over, what they talk about, what they say about the television programs you watch. Anything you can think of, just write it down. You're free to write what you like. Now — one, two, three...start!"

"Can I erase?" asked a boy.

"Yes," said the captain.

"Can I write with a ballpoint pen?" asked another.

"Yes, boy, of course."

"Can I use a sheet with little squares?" asked a girl.

"Perfect," answered the captain.

"Sir, how much do we have to write?" asked another boy.

"Two or three pages."

"Two or three pages!" groaned the children.

"Very well," replied the captain. "One or two, then. Now, write!" he bellowed.

The children sucked on their pencils and looked up at the ceiling to see if some ideas might come flying down into their heads.

Pedro was chewing his pencil, but he couldn't think of even one word. He picked his nose. A tiny snot came out by mistake and he put it under his desk. At the next desk, Juan was biting his nails one by one.

"Do you eat them?" asked Pedro.

"What?" said Juan.

"Your nails."

"No. I cut them with my teeth and then I spit them out. Like this. See?"

The captain walked down the aisle, and Pedro could see his hard, shiny gold belt buckle.

"You two! Aren't you working?" he said.

"Yes, sir," said Juan, and he wrinkled his eyebrows, stuck his tongue between his teeth and wrote a big "A" to start his composition. When the captain walked back toward the blackboard to talk to the teacher, Pedro looked over at Juan's sheet.

"What are you going to write?" he asked.

"Anything," said Juan. "How about you?"

"I don't know," said Pedro.

"What did your parents do yesterday?" asked Juan.

"Same as usual. They came home, they ate, they listened to the radio, they went to bed."

"Just like my mother."

"My mother started crying," said Pedro.

"Mothers are always crying," said Juan.

"I hardly ever cry," said Pedro. "I haven't cried for a year."

"What about if I hit you and you get a black eye. Would you cry then?" asked Juan.

"Why would you do that when you're my friend?" said Pedro.

"That's true. I wouldn't," answered Juan.

The boys put their pencils in their mouths again and looked at the burnt-out lightbulb and the shadows on the wall. Pedro felt as if his head was as empty as a piggy bank with no money in it. He leaned over to Juan and whispered in his ear, "Are you against the dictatorship?"

Juan looked up to see where the captain was and leaned toward Pedro. "Of course, stupid."

Pedro moved away and winked, smiling. Then, pretending to write, he said, "But you're a child."

"So what?" answered Juan.

"My mother said that children..." began Pedro.

"They all say that," said Juan. "They took my father away up north."

"Just like Daniel," said Pedro.

"Yeah, just like Daniel."

Pedro looked down at what he had written on his paper: *What My Family Does at Night by Pedro Malbrán, Siria School, Grade Three A.*

"Juan, if I win the medal I'm going to sell it to buy a size five soccer ball made of leather with black patches," he said. Then he wet his pencil lead with a bit of spit, took a deep breath and wrote: *When my father comes home from work...*

A week went by. A tree in the square fell down because it was so old. The garbage truck didn't come for five days and flies buzzed around people's eyes. Gustavo Martínez, who lived across the street, got married and the neighbors shared his wedding cake. The jeep came back and took Manuel Pedraza, the teacher, to jail. The priest didn't want to say Sunday mass.

On the school wall the word Resistance appeared. Daniel played soccer again and scored two goals. The price of an ice cream cone went up, and Matilde Schepp, who turned nine years old, asked Pedro to kiss her on the mouth.

"You're crazy!" yelled Pedro.

After that week had gone by, another passed, too, and then one day the captain came back to the classroom. He was carrying lots of sheets of paper and a calendar with a picture of General Perdomo on it. His pocket was bulging with candies.

"My dear young friends," he said, "your compositions were very nice and they made us soldiers very happy. On behalf of my colleagues and General Perdomo, I want to congratulate you very sincerely. The gold medal was not won by your class, but by another class. But to reward your nice little essays, I will give each of you a candy and your composition with a comment on it. This calendar with the picture of our leader is for your classroom."

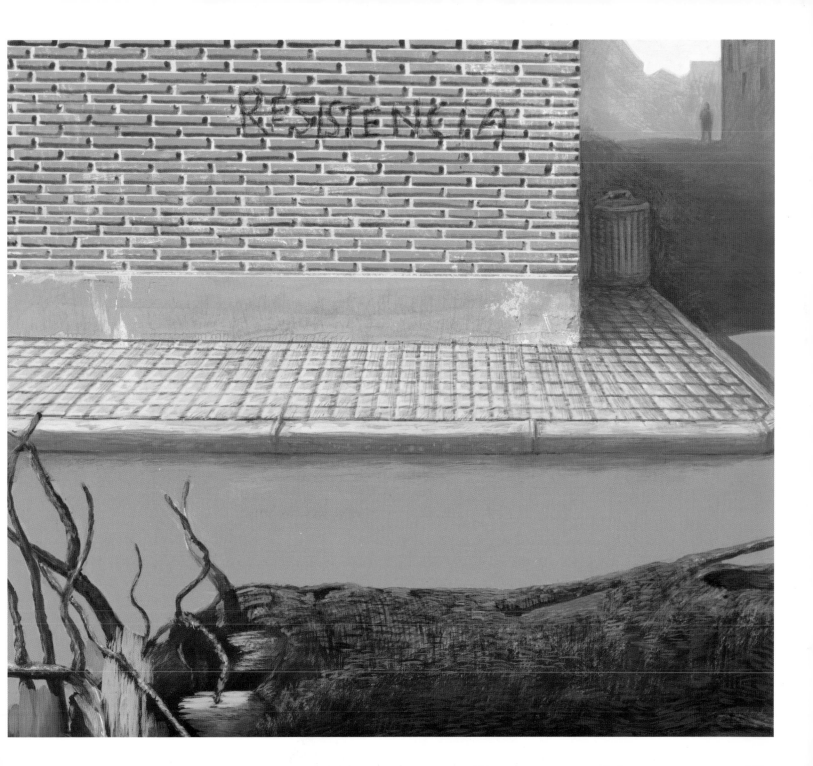

Pedro ate his candy on the way home. During supper that night he said to his father, "In school they made us write a composition."

"Mmm. What about?" asked his father as he ate his soup.

"What our family does at night," Pedro answered.

Father's spoon fell on his plate and splashed some soup onto the tablecloth. He looked at Pedro's mother.

"And what did you write, son?" she asked.

Pedro left the table and went to look through his notebooks.

"Do you want me to read it to you? The captain congratulated me." He showed them where the captain had written in ink, "Bravo! I congratulate you."

"The captain! What captain?" yelled his father.

"The one who made us write the composition," explained Pedro.

His parents looked at each other again and Pedro began to read, "Siria School, Grade Three A —"

"Just read what it says, okay?" his father interrupted.

And while his parents listened carefully, Pedro read.

What My Family Does at Night by Pedro Malbrán,
Siria School, Grade Three A

When my father comes home from work, I wait
for him at the bus stop. Sometimes my mother is
at home, and when my father comes in, she says What's
up kid, what happened today? Fine, says my father, and how
about you? Then I go out and play soccer. I like scoring
headers. Then comes my mother and says, Pedrito come
and eat and we sit at the table and I eat everything
except soup because I don't like it. After supper every
night my father and mother sit on the sofa and play chess
and I do my homework. And they go on playing chess until
it's time to go to bed. After that I don't know because
I am asleep.

Signed: Pedro Malbrán.

Note: If you give me the prize for this composition I
hope it's a soccer ball but not a plastic one.

When my father comes home from work, I wait for him at the bus stop. Sometimes my mother is at home, and when my father comes in, she says, What's up, kid, what happened today? Fine, says my father, and how about you? Then I go out and play soccer. I like scoring headers. Then comes my mother and says, Pedrito come and eat and we sit at the table and I eat everything except soup because I don't like it. After supper every night my father and mother sit on the sofa and play chess and I do my homework. And they go on playing chess until it's time to go to bed. After that I don't know because I'm asleep. Signed — Pedro Malbrán.

Note: If you give me the prize for this composition I hope it's a soccer ball but not a plastic one.

Pedro looked up and saw that his parents were smiling.

"Well," said his father, "we'd better buy a chess set."

Dictatorship

In some countries of the world, people live under a dictatorship, where an individual or a small group of people hold all the power. They run the country as they want, without considering the wishes of the people. In a dictatorship, it is not possible for people to influence how the government acts or even to change it. Courts, elections, legislatures (such as Congress or Parliament) and political parties either don't exist or have no real power.

In a dictatorship, there is no freedom of speech or freedom of the press. People who demonstrate against the dictatorship can be arrested simply because they disagree with the government.

Dictatorships stay in power by eliminating or controlling the people who oppose them. To do this, they must find out exactly who is against them. So they may encourage and reward people who reveal what their neighbors and families are doing. Sometimes they even try to get children to tell on their own parents, which is what happens to Pedro in *The Composition*.

Dictatorships frighten people into obeying them through the use of torture, imprisonment and sometimes even killing their opponents. They usually have large police forces and rely on the army to enforce their rule. The dictators themselves often come from the army.

Despite the power of dictators, people do struggle against them. They can secretly try to organize resistance movements, even in the face of danger. They can also seek help from other countries and from organizations such as the United Nations, and in time they can defeat dictators and restore democracy to their countries.